THE ADVENTURES OF SARAH SIMMONS

Sarah Simmons was a young girl. Well she was actually sixteen so she classified herself as an adult. These are the many adventures in the life of Sarah Simmons.

Hello, my name is Sarah. I'm sixteen and a typical teenager. Except for the fact that I am able to see hear and do things that normal girls can't do. I have a dog named Mizu; a cat named Whiskers and lives in a house that is magical. And am home schooled by a very strange man named Mr. Wickem. My mother and father are in Africa so I am currently living with him. It's his house that's magical. It's pretty cool.

Oh God, morning again. Yippy…I'm going back to bed. "Knock Knock, Sarah, are you up yet? It's time for your lessons." Great, time for a healthy dose of algebra. Fun. Mr. Wickem who I fondly call Wiki (He hates it) was waiting for me downstairs textbook in hand. "Look who has finally graced us with her presence". He's an older man, in his sixty's. He's pretty cool. "It's too early for lessons" I say as I yawn. "It's never too early to learn something, besides its twelve o'clock. Why don't you get something from the fridge?" I love our fridge. All you have to do is tell it what you want, open it and "Bam" there it is. "I would like a Smirnoff Green Apple" "Bam, ID Please" Damn, that never works. "Okay, I would like a Dr. Pepper and a Frito Pie." "Bam" Nice.

As I go into the kitchen past the moving photographs of Wiki's family I see Wiki sitting in the parlor, green robe, slippers and pipe. Whiskers, my calico cat sat next to him on the sofa drinking out of his coffee cup. I have no idea where Mizu is. She's a dachshund by the way. "Okay" Wiki says " Lets try something new today." Great, more school work. He always is coming up with new ways to torture me. "What is it this time" He looks at me like he always does when I resist a new lesson (one eye quirked and his nose all scrunched). "Today" he continues with a pause for effect "We will try to dissect something." Oh, great and gross I hate cutting up dead things. I can't even slice a fish for dinner. He leaves the room for a minuet and comes back with something resembling a lizard. "What is that" I ask. "This is a baby dragon" Wiki said as he places it on the table. "A WHAT" I yell in shock.

"It's a baby dragon" He says again. "They're real" I say, still in complete shock. "Of coarse they're real. There's one right there on the table. Can't you see" I look at him like he's a lunatic and he looks right back at me as if I'm just as crazy. "Okay, let's hop to it then. Grab the scalpel."

An hour later as I'm wiping green slime off my hands, I ponder the events of that day. Scales, wings, long pointed tongue. By George, I think that really was a dragon. Weird, very weird.

The next day Wiki woke me up extra early. "Today" He says smiling as he holds a towel "We are going to take a trip to the beach" "No class" I yelp as I jump right up! In two second flat, I'm ready to go. I have on a hot pink bikini with a black skull on it, black flip flops, and sunglasses. He's wearing an old fashioned red striped swimsuit, snorkel and mask. "Ready to go" He asks me through the snorkel. I nod my head vigorously and we're off.

We arrive at the beach around noon, and I can smell the salty air. "Wow, this is great" I say while stretching my arms to the sky. "It's been age's since I've been here" Wiki replies. He's still wearing the mask, by the way. LOL. "For today's lesson..." He starts to say, before I rudely cut him off. "Wait what, I thought today was going to be a vacation". "It is but..." "There's always time to learn something" I finish his sentence. "Precisely" he finishes. I knew this vacation was too good to be true. As I turn to look at him I can't stop myself from laughing. Picture this, white haired man in a funny looking swimsuit wearing snorkel, mask and big floppy flippers. He then precedes to hand me a pair of my own. "Put these on" I look at him as if he's crazy. "Put these on. We're going for a swim." I was planning on working on my tan, but apparently I'm going seaweed diving instead.

"I look ridicules" I grumble as I march into the waves. Actually it doesn't matter how I look because there isn't anybody around to see me anyway. We are at a very deserted part of the beach. The place where we are at is very isolated behind thick palm trees. "Damn, the waters cold" I say with a slight shiver. "You'll get used to it" He calls as he jumps right in. He swims past the waves into the deep water. "Wait for me" I yell, trying to be louder than the oceans roar. "So what's the agenda for today" I ask as I finally catch up to him. "We're looking for mermaids" This time not only do I look at him as if he's crazy, but I actually think he is.

Okay, maybe I'm in denial about living with a lunatic for the past three years, but to quote Wiki "Anything's Possible if you just believe". So, I guess I'll just go with it. We swim awhile and I see a fin poking out from behind a rock. "Oh, look a mermaid" I say sarcastically. "Don't be silly Sarah, that's a blowfish" Apparently he thinks I'M stupid. Wiki dives down to the ocean bottom (We're in a more shallow area where the water is crystal clear). He comes up holding a huge sand dollar. "We're close" He says. "Close to what" I reply. "To the mermaids" He says gesturing to the sand dollar as if he thinks it's proof. I roll my eyes but go along with it. "This sand dollar is the common currency for the mer-people…Don't you rolls those eyes at me again Sarah." "It's a sea creature" I say. (We are above the water level by the way, just incase you thought we were speaking fish or something.) "Of coarse it's a living sea creature. Do you honestly think that they would use dead ones? It'd be like bartering with a corps" he says. "Wow, thanks for putting that lovely image into my head." I roll my eyes again. He ignores it. "Quick put your head under water" He says as he dunks my head under. I was about to swim up all pissed off, when I hear something. It's like an eerie little singing sound. It's kind of pretty. I'm actually beginning to consider the possibility of there actually being mermaids, when something with fins swiftly swims past me. 'Oh my God, a mermaid' I think as I turn around. I begin to smile until I see a big grey body and teeth.

"Ahhh!!! It's a Shark" I scream as I quickly swim to the top and then flutter about in panic. Wiki doesn't appear to be as excited as I am. He remains quite calm, actually. "What's wrong with you" I scream "There's a shark and it's right next to me" He motions to go back under water. Reluctantly I do, and I see colorful fins and lots of hair swimming all around me. I stare in awe as I see a beautiful young woman who happens to have a tail, starring right at me. The sharks gone and she motions for me to come to her. I do and she puts something in my hand. I look to see that it's a shark tooth, and I look back up but she's gone. I come back above water and I see Wiki smiling at me. "I told you so" he says with a twinkle in his eye, and then we swim back. When we get back to shore my legs feel all tingly. Must be from all the swimming. The sun is about to set so we get in the car and watch it go down. "What a beautiful sight" I say. "Indeed it is" he replies. Today turned out to be a wonderful vacation after all.

It's been two weeks since the mermaid incident. Lessons have been going on as usual (Boring as usual as well). Yesterday we studied anatomy. Gross. I actually prefer dissecting dragons. It's raining right now and I am so bored. The rain makes it extra boring. Whiskers is lying on my lap purring slightly, and Mizu is outside trying to eat raindrops. Our yard looks like a jungle. Wiki is a terrible gardener. 'I like to keep the yard looking natural' is what he always says. I think that's just an excuse for being lazy. He doesn't even do dishes. Well, it's actually kind of cool. They kind of do themselves. That is not just a metaphor. I'm getting kind of hungry so I go to the fridge. Whiskers complains loudly. I think I've found a way to get that Smirnoff. I used my recourses to get a fake ID. "I would like a Smirnoff green apple" 'Bam' 'ID please' I was ready for that one. "Here you go" I say slipping in my fake ID. Man, am I good or what. 'Bam' 'Nice try, that looks nothing like you' damn it, I really thought I had it fooled. I give up. "Fine, give me a veggie pizza with onion rings and a root beer float." 'Bam' "What the...Salad and is that carrot juice?" I am so pissed. I am not eating rabbit food, and I think the refrigerator just called me fat. Grrrr. As I leave the kitchen I notice Wiki staring out the window. "It's stopped raining" He says as he turns around. "Yup" I say, glaring at my salad. "Come on get in the car, we're going for a ride". "Why" I ask. "There's a rainbow" he says pointing upward. "And…" "We're going to follow it" he replies. Oh God, here we go again.

Okay, so we've been on the road for about an hour and a half. The rainbow is continuous. It seems like it will never end. I am so bored. Suddenly the car pulls over. "Thank God, my legs were starting to cramp" I say stretching. "We'll have to follow the rest of it on foot" Wiki says pointing to a dreary looking wood. "I am not going in there. It's creepy and muddy. I'll get my shoes dirty." I say this while I cross my arms over my chest. "Oh look, there's a friendly looking skunk" Wiki says pointing at my feet. "Ahhh! Let's go right now" I yell behind me, halfway into the forest.

We walk for a mile or so until we stop at a clearing. "Look, we're here" Wiki says. He then proceeds to walk behind a rock and pulls something out. It appears to be some kind of bucket. I look inside and I see something gold and shiny. "Oh my God, I'm rich" I scream. Grabbing for the gold. I'm thinking of all the cool things I am now wealthy enough to buy. (A car, a flat

screen TV, A complete entertainment system, I could even buy a house.) As I grab a hold of a gold nugget someone taps me from behind. "Umm, that would be mine" says a strange little man in green. "I found it first" I say clutching the gold tightly. "Yes, but I put it there" the man says. "Sarah, that's a leprechaun" Wiki says. I take a closer look and I think he's right. The little man has on a green suit, has red curly hair, and a red curly beard. Plus he speaks with an Irish accent. "If you don't mind I'll be having that back now" the leprechaun says, snatching away my gold. "Damn it! I thought I was going to be rich" I grumble. "Well you did come all this way. I guess I could be giving you something" the leprechaun says as he hands me a small gold nugget.
"Thank you" I say, and in an instant he was gone. Man that little dude is fast.

As Wiki and I drive home my hands and arms get all tingly. I tell Wiki about it but he shrugs it off. "It's probably just from touching leprechaun gold" he says. "So, what's on tomorrows agenda" I ask. "Tomorrow we are going to find and study fairies." Wiki says. Yup, He's crazy. He really is I think to myself, as we drive the rest of the way home in silence.

"Beep beep beep" Ugh, my alarm is so annoying. Its nine am, and a Saturday none the less. I never get a break. I slowly get out of bed and stretch. I can smell bacon burning downstairs. I guess Wiki decided to cook breakfast the old fashioned way. As I head downstairs think about what Wiki had said. Fairies aren't real are they, that's absurd. Then again I have seen mermaids and leprechauns. Maybe they are real. When I get downstairs I see Wiki at the table holding and eating a piece of burnt bacon with peanut butter on the side. Ewww, he really does have a very weird appetite. "Bacon" he offers. "No thank you" I reply. "So, what's the plan for today" I ask. "We are going to find and study fairies" he says with a mouthful of bacon. "Yes, but how" I questioned, not believing I actually just asked that. "We are going to alter our eyesight so that we can see them in their own environment" He answers. "Naturally" I say, trying to humor him. He gets up from the table and beckons for me to follow him outside. I follow him to the garden. It's messy as usual. Wiki taps me on the shoulder and as I turn around he shoves a big old fashioned flash camera in my face. It goes off blinding me. "WHAT THE HELL!!! WHAT WAS THAT FOR" I screech. "I was altering your eyes" he replies calmly. "I'm seeing spots" I complain, rubbing my eyes. "That's the point. Those spots that you see aren't really spots at all. They are in fact the aura of fairies. Look closely" He says handing me a magnifying glass. I grab it and take a closer look. I can't believe what I see. In front of me is a tiny little girl. She hovers before me with tiny little translucent wings. "Close your mouth Sarah. It's not ladylike." Wiki remarks. I continue to stare in amazement. "Is she a fairy" I ask, still in shock. "She is indeed" he replies smiling. The little creature flutters about in front of me then lands on my nose. I sneeze, and as quick as you can say 'chimmy changa' she's gone. "Where did she go" I ask, looking around wildly. "Oh, you know fairies. They can't stay in one place for too long. They get bored" Wiki casually answers. Then he goes inside without as much as a second thought of the matter. I stay outside. I can't believe what just happened. I actually saw a real live fairy. My face is still tingly where she touched me. I have a bit of a headache so I get excused from lessons and go to bed.

I wake up to a slow steady beeping. 'That's not my alarm clock' I think to myself as I open my eyes. "Look, she's awake" a mans voice says, and I turn to see that it's my father. "Dad, what are you doing here" I ask in confusion. As I look at my surroundings I realize that I'm in a hospital room. I see my mother and father looking at me with tears in their eyes. "It's a miracle. You've come back to us." Mom says. "We thought we'd lost you" Dad finishes. "What the hell is going on? Aren't you guys supposed to be in Africa? What's happened" I nearly yell in confusion. "Honey, you've been in a coma for three and a half years. You just barely woke up" Dad says as he hugs me for what feels like hours. My head is spinning. Was it all just a dream? Did I imagine Wiki and all the adventures I went on. I'm snapped back to reality by a knock on the door. I turn to see who it is and my jaw drops. "Baby, meet the wonderful doctor who saved your life. Mr. James Albert Wikkam." Mom says pointing to Wiki. "I'm glad to see that you're finally up" He says with a wink. "Remember, anything is possible if you just believe."

THE END

Authors note

This story is about opening your mind, and living in your imagination.

Anything is possible. I may have experienced something like what Sarah experienced. I was in a coma when I was twelve. I pulled out of it and now pray for everyone in that situation. I would like to believe that those people are in some sort of happy magical world instead of one of pain and torture.

IGNORED

This is a story of a girl who was terribly ignored.

Hello, my name is Alyssa Adams. I'm sixteen and might as well be invisible. No one at school talks to me except for my best friend Catherine. And of all people, she's head cheerleader, year book editor, and captain of our debate team. Needless to say she's pretty popular. Needless to say I'm not. I don't even know why she even talks to me. I'm so unpopular I might as well be invisible. I'm so unpopular I might as well be dead.

" Di do di dum 'Good morning' Dum di do di do" Ahh! That stupid alarm clock. I've had it since I was five. I want to get rid of it, but I just can't bring myself to through it away. Oh well, time to get up for another glorious day at Alexander High. As I walk out my bedroom door I smell the overwhelming scent of cigarette smoke. I cough slightly then walk down stairs. I see my mother passed out on the kitchen table cigarette still in hand. Mom's been binge drinking again I see. She hasn't always been like this. She used to be quite productive, always keeping busy. Now she barely baths, drinks all the time and when she's not drunk she's sleeping it off. 'Mother what's happened to you' I think to myself. I shake my head and then run out the door where Catharine is waiting.

"Hey Cat, what's kicking" I say trying to give her a hug. "Stop that Alyssa, people will think that we're gay" she laughs. "When did you become the little homophobe" I joke. We continue on until we get to school. " Well I got to book. Don't want to be late to snore, I mean math class" Cat says waving. " Can' t stand to bee seen with me huh Cat" I yell after her laughing. But, I kind of mean it.

As I walk to first period no one even looks at me. No one says hello. It's like no one even knows that I'm alive. And, I'm not even new here. Most of these people have known me since elementary school. It's sad when not even they will wave, nod, or at least smile at you. I wasn't always this unpopular. I don't know what could have happened. I just have the worst luck.

" A minus X divided by three is equal to… Anyone?" Mr. Bell asks. He's my algebra teacher by the way. “Twenty two” I say, halfway raising my hand. “Twenty two, people you know this. Hasn’t anyone been doing the homework?” I just said that. “What is 12x divided by 3” he continues without even hearing me. “Nine” I say. “Nine” The guy behind me copies. “Good job Mr. Blake. You see, jocks can be smart too” Mr. Bell says, and the class laughs along. Everyone laughs, except me that is. I’m pissed. I’m even invisible to the teachers. I raise my hand. “Sir, may I go to the bathroom.” He ignores me. “Sir” I say a little louder “May I be excused” . Still no response. I raise my hand a little higher and speak a little louder. “ Sir, may I please be excused to use the bathroom” He obviously doesn’t care so I just go.

I go to the bathroom and then go to my locker. For some reason for the past couple of weeks my lockers been broken. It hasn’t been able to open no matter what I do. Tomorrow I’m thinking of coming to school with a crow bar. Campus police probably wouldn’t even notice.

The bell for lunch rings so I go to the feeding trough where all the cattle meet. Can’t find Catherine, nope…there she is. I wave to her and she beckons for me to come out side with her. It’s like she doesn’t want to be seen in public with me or something. “My locker still won’t open” I say as I come to sit by her. “ Oh…Hey, was algebra a snore” she fakes a yawn. “Very funny” I say. “But seriously, why do you want to eat outside” “The cafeterias too noisy” she replies. “ Yeah right, you just don’t want to be seen with me” I tease, but she looks kind of hurt. But in a second she’s over it and talking again as usual. “Do you want to come over after school” I ask as I try to steal a fry from he plate. She moves her plate. “Sorry, can’t I have a doctors appointment remember.” “Again, What’s wrong with you? This is the third one this week” I say concerned. “Oh, it’s nothing. Hey, I’m going to the bathroom. I’ll be right back.” She says quickly then she gets up and walks off. Strange, very strange. As I look down I see that she’s dropped something. It’s a business card for the Hope Counseling center. Cat’s in therapy? What could be so bad in her life that she needs therapy? “Hey, I’m back” She says as she comes up. Then she looks at my hand. “ Where did you find that” she asks. Her face is very serious. “ It fell out of your bag. When were you going to tell me about this” I say trying to grab her hand. She pulls away “ It’s nothing, look I got to go. If you want to talk meet me by the big oak tree at the park near your house tonight at seven. If you want to talk we can talk then. I’ll see you later.” “Cat, wait” I say, but she’s already gone.

I am so upset I don't even bother to go to class. I just go strait home. My moms sleeping on the couch bottle in hand. "Mom I'm home" I say as I turn off the TV. "Alyssa your back" my mom says faintly. "Yeah, school was terrible" I say but she had already gone back to sleep. Never mind. My brothers home. I can hear the loud music coming from his room. Hardcore something or other. He just barely started listing to it. It's all he listens to now. All he ever does now is stay in his room. He won't even talk to me. We used to be so close. He's only a year younger than me. It's sad how family's fall apart.

It's seven now and it's getting dark. I'm by the big oak tree and it's cold out. I should have brought a jacket. Here comes Catherine. " Hey sorry I'm late." What else is new. "So are you going to tell me what's up or what" I ask. "Come on, lets take a walk" she says. "So" I say. "So what" she replies. "So are you going to tell me why your in therapy three times a week or do I have to guess" I finish. "Something happened about a month ago." Catherine says softly. "Yeah, you totaled your brand new car. Hardly cause for therapy" It was a joke but Cat's not laughing. " Oh God, you really loved that car didn't you." Catherine smiles sadly and nods. " Do you remember anything about that day" Cat asks me voice quivering. " Sure, I got up, had breakfast went to school…" I say, trying to remember. "And after school…"
She pry's. " We went to a party…we drank a little…we were driving home and then…" "And then we crashed" Cat finishes tears in her eyes. We've stopped now. I look around. I do a double take and then start to freak out. " Cat…why are we at a cemetery" She's really crying now as she points to a stone. It's engraved ' In loving memory of a wonderful girl Alyssa Adams Born 6-7-1993 Died 9-29-2009 She was loved by everyone' " …what…this can't be…I'm not dead…I can't be…Catherine, you can see me right. I'm not dead. I'm right here. Stop crying" I try to give he a hug. This time she doesn't move away. I fall strait trough her. Catherine's hysterical. " It's all my fault, it's all MY FAULT!!! If I hadn't been drinking none of this would have happened. You DIED because of ME! YOUR GONE because of ME!!!" I can't calm her down. I can't calm ME down. Cat's banging her head against my tombstone, shouldn't I be the one upset? "Catherin calm down. Please calm down" Now I'm crying. That's why my moms always drunk and my brothers into that music. To hide the pain. That's why nobody

notices me. I'm not unpopular, I'm just Dead…Not like that's any better. But still at least I'm not hated or invisible. Look at me all Polly Anna Looking on the bright side. For being dead I'm pretty cheerful.

Oh God, I think it's just hit me. I'm Dead. I'm not coming back. I'm gone forever. No more Dr. Pepper -n- Gummy worms, no more boyfriends, no more school (actually I'm not too sad about the last part)No more anything. I'm Gone. What am I going to do now? Well, first I have to help Catherine. "Cat snap out of it" She stops crying and listens. "You made a mistake, you killed me but I'm still here" She laughs a little than sniffles. " You need to pull yourself together and move on. I know I'm going to have to. But, I can't do that until I help you." She hiccups. We both laugh. "Alyssa, what are you going to do now" she asks sniffling. " I don't know I reply" As I say that I start to feel lightheaded, then warm, and then I see something bright and shiny coming closer and closer. " I see a light Cat, what should I do?" I ask her. " I think you need to go" she replies. "But before you do I just wanted to say I was sorry" "For what" I ask. "Umm…For killing you" "Oh, right…well all is forgiven. And I'm sorry for puking all over your brand new skirt when I had the stomach flu." We both laugh. "All is forgiven" she says. "Tell my mother I love her. And tell my brother not to give her a hard time" I say. "I Promise" she said crossing her heart. "I'll never forget you" she says. " You'd better not. I love you Catherine. You're my best friend." "I love you too" I feel like I'm rising. Everything starts to fade away. I feel happy. I feel at peace. I wasn't ignored. I wasn't invisible. I was loved. I am loved.

AN EIRE TALE

Hello, my name is Elena Rigby. I'm twenty one years old and am on a mission. I'm on a mission to find my twin sister Eire. She has been kidnapped by a cult. She's been gone since I was six. We are identical twins. We both have black hair and blue eyes. The last time I saw her we were in pig tails. Now I don't now how she looks. All I know is that she looks just like me. After she was taken things went bad, really bad. My parents had been members of the organization of The Children of the Sun and the Moon Church. They were in it since college. That's actually how they met. You know how people fall in love, date, get purposed to romantically, and then marry? That was not the case for mom and dad. They were "matched". Basically it was decided by their church leader, whom they worshiped and thought was God. He just pointed at her and at him in the crowd, put his hands together and "bang" they were engaged. They didn't even know each other. But they bought into it, clearly or else I wouldn't be here. They got married just a couple of months after they were matched. But, do you want to know the weirdest part? They weren't allowed to live together or even consummate their marriage until they completed three years of missionary work. They didn't go help aids orphans in Africa though. They would go door to door with pamphlets and sell flowers by the freeway to raise money for the church. They weren't bad people, though. They were just naive and terribly confused. My sister and I were conceived right after they got together. It was a difficult labor for my mother. She was in labor for twenty three hours. I was born April 1st 1988 at twelve' o 'two in the morning. My sister was born March 31st at eleven fifty-eight at night. We are only four minutes apart, but we have two different birthdays. It's weird. But then again, what part of my story isn't? My sister and I have always been close. We have a very special bond. We are identical twins, after all. When we were babies we lived in the church house. We lived there till I was about five. There were a lot of people living there with us. It was sort of a boarding house/ apartment complex. There were plenty of kids for us to play with, but my sister and I kept to ourselves mostly. We would play hide and seek a lot. We would play mirrors which is a game where you stand in front of each other, put our hands and feet together and do exactly what the other one does. Anyone can play it, but it's more fun when you're playing it with someone who looks exactly like you. We really used to freak people out doing that. My sister and I even came up with our own little language. To everyone else it sounded like gibberish, but it made sense to us. We had so much fun together. I hate those people for taking her away from me. It was a stormy night in October. I remember that we were scared, because we heard noises. It sounded like some sort of weird chanting. We huddled up under our cabbage patch comforter and tried to be invisible. Just then three men in black hooded robes burst through the door. They were really scary. They grabbed Eire. She tried to hold on to me, but they pried her away. She was kicking and screaming. They put a hood over her face to muffle her sobs. I tried to fight them. I was trying to protect her, but they were just too strong. I felt so helpless. I didn't know what to do. Where were my mother and father? How could they let this happen? I was so angry and confused. I went to live with my aunt after that. My parents wanted nothing to do with me. You would think that losing one daughter would make them love me more, but no. That was not the case. They sent me away. The last thing that my mother said to me was "She's in a better place now".

In sixth grade I started hearing voices. I would see things too. But they weren't neon rabbits or weirs shit like that. I would see her. I would hear her voice. I was standing alone in the hallway of my school. Suddenly a girl that looked just like me ran past. I knew that it was her. I knew that it was my sister. I followed her to the gym. I went behind the big curtain where the drama club keeps their stuff. "Elena… Elena" a voice just like mine called out. "Eire, I'm here. Where are you" I cried desperately. I followed the voice to a curtain. "I've found you" I say as I pull it back. But to my utter dismay it was only my own reflecting starring back at me. I was so angry and disappointed that I punched the mirror. It shattered and I was left alone, and bleeding in the dark.

In ninth grade I found a note crumpled up in my locker. All it said was "On the shores of lake Eire..". That got my attention immediately. I looked everywhere for the person who wrote the note. That was note was my only clue to finding her. Fate would tease me like that, often. I would hear her singing when I was in the shower. I would jump out and look, but there was no one there. I would see little girls playing at the park. Sometimes they would be playing tag or maybe fighting over a doll. They reminded me so much of my sister. I had lost complete contact with my parents. They, along with they're crazy church had moved. I had no Idea where I could find them. I looked up The Children of the Sun and the Moon on the internet, but found no reference. I'm always on the lookout for clues to find her. I dropped out of school and ran away to New York. That's the last place I saw her.

"I want a shot of vodka on the rocks, and make it a double". That would be the fifth shot I would be taking today. There has been no progress on finding Eire. I find it easy to take comfort in the warm and fuzzy feeling of alcoholism. Getting drunk is the only way to silence the voices of my guilty conscience. I'm about to order another round when some man I don't know comes up to me. "Eire, what are you doing here? You know you're not supposed to drink." He says, putting his hand on my shoulder. "What did you just call me" I ask in utter shock. "Oh, I'm sorry. I thought that you were someone else." The man says and then walks out the door and down the street. I run after him, completely forgetting to pay my bar tab. I chase him down an alley. "Wait" I scream after him. Many heads turn but I take no notice. My eyes are only on him. I finally catch up to him and grab a hold of his arm. He tries desperately to free himself from my grasp, so I punch him in the face. He falls to the ground and I straddle him, sitting on his stomach. He looks completely freaked, but I don't care. "Who are you, and what can you tell me about my sister?" I growl, pulling him up by the collar. "I... I... My name is Thomas Evans, and I mistook you for someone else." He stammers. "I know that, now where's Eire? Where do you know her from?" I question. "We are apart of the same church. We sell flowers together sometimes. Please let me go. I can't help you" he answers. "Like hell you can't help me. Tell me what I need to know, now. I'm drunk and can not be held responsible for my actions." I threaten, starting to get irritated. "You need serious help lady. My church group meets at this address every Wednesday evening. Maybe they can help you. "He says handing me a card. I get off him and let him go. He runs off quicker than a gazelle runs from a hungry lion. I stand there still in shock. Is this it? Have I finally found her? I'm so close to her, yet I don't want to get my hopes up. This may be it. I may have finally found my sister. I am so excites I throw up, and then pass out.

I wake up in the alley, with a bad taste in my mouth and throw up on my blouse. I hurry home to change. I unlock my apartment and turn on the lights. It's a tiny one bedroom. I don't have much furniture, It kind of looks like I just moved in; even though I've lived here for three years already. I don't make friends. I'm scarred of getting close to people. When I lost my sister I lost everything. I take a quick shower then throw on a tee-shirt and a pair of jeans. I brush my hair and look at myself in the mirror. I pretend that I'm looking at Eire. Maybe soon I really will be looking at her.

I drive to the address on the card. It's an old looking building. It looks like it needs to be condemned, actually. Is this where she's been? Poor Eire, this place look like hell. I knock on the big door, but don't wait for anyone to answer. I let myself in and step into the corridor. It's lit with candles. It's creepy and smells of incense and mold. I walk down the hall till I hear chanting. I freeze, standing there quietly. My body goes tense. It's the exact same sound I heard all those years ago. I'm really scared, but I can't stop now. I follow the noise to a big auditorium. There are a bunch of people gathered in a circle. In the middle is something covered with a big cloth? All of a sudden they all turn to look at me. "She's here" say in some creepy kind of unison. Okay, I'm really scarred now. "Where is she" I ask, demanding an answer. "Where is who my dear?" An older man asks. Are they really going to play dumb with me? "We have something to show you" a woman says beckoning for me to come closer. I look in the direction that they are pointing, and to my complete surprise my parents step out of the shadows. "Mom, Dad Eire's been with you the whole time?" I ask in confusion. "Darling you are Eire." My dad replies. They pull the cloth back to reveal a mirror. I look into it but see only myself. I am tripping out. "What do you mean, are you crazy?" I say backing away slowly. "I was pregnant with twins, but you were born an only child." My mother answers stepping towards me. "What are you talking about, she's real. She's not just in my head" I cry, starting to shake. "Of coarse she's real.

Her spirit lives in your body. She's like a split personality" My father says. "No, I can't cope with this." I lunge toward the big mirror and throw myself into it. Pieces of glass cut my skin. A big piece slits my throat. As I lay on the ground bleeding I see her. She's standing over me hand outstretched. I take her hand as I close my eyes. We are finally together. I'm finally at peace. And I slowly slip away into nothingness.

I got this idea for this story from a real life experience; my parents were part of the Unification Church Aka: The Moonie Cult. They got out of it. But they were matched. I also really have a thing for twins. I've always wanted one. This is a very morbid story from a weird mind. I hope that you liked it.

THE BEAUTIFUL PEOPLE OF LOVELY LAKE

Have you ever felt like you don't fit in? Have you ever felt like you don't belong? Have you ever felt self conscientious about what you wear? If you answered yes to any of these questions, you are among the many teenage young adults who suffer from low self esteem. Barbie Holiday is not one of these people.

Barbie Holiday was a typical sixteen year-old girl. She had long beautiful blonde hair, bright blue eyes, and long luscious legs. She was tall with a great tan and perfect teeth. She was the most popular girl in school. She was hot and she knew it. She never had a care in the world. That is all about to change in about ten seconds.

"WHAT DO YOU MEAN WE'RE MOVING?" Barbie screamed, almost at the top of her lungs. She didn't have to worry about waking the neighbors because her house was thirteen acres away from everyone. She lived in a big house in the richest part of town. It was only five minutes from the beach, the mall and her favorite sushi bar. She had it made. "Your dad got transferred to Michigan, honey, please calm down." Mrs. Holiday pleaded, hand outstretched towards her daughter. "I will not calm down! My whole life is here! How can you expect me to just pick up and start over in measly old Michigan" Blondie continued, nearly hysterical. "Oh, come now. You're a beautiful young girl. You'll adjust in no time." Mr. Holiday said, stepping towards his daughter. "It's not fair. Daddy, I don't want to go" Barbie cried. She felt very sorry for herself. Poor Barbie sulked around the house for the next two weeks, packing up her home and ignoring the attempts her parents made to cheer her up. Barbie's Dad left the week before to ready the house and start his new job. Barbie and her mother followed the week after with the movers.

When Barbie arrived in Lovely Lake, her first thoughts were how quaint the little town was. It had a lot of tall trees. They were piney, and made her nose itch. They were tall and even a bit sinister looking, that is if you had a suspicious mind. However, there was no lake in sight. There probably was one at one time but not anymore.

“I don’t want to go to school today” Barbie whined at the breakfast table. “Honey, you’ll do fine. You’re ahead in your class and you’re very pretty. You’ll make friends in no time.” Mrs. Holiday said, trying to comfort her sulking daughter. Barbie looked at her mother for a minute. She was an older woman, mid forties. She had wrinkles on her face and limp, chin length brown hair. She was sort of plain looking. Barbie couldn’t figure out where she got her good looks from. Her father looked just as plain and was overweight and balding a little. “Hurry up and finish your breakfast dear. You’ll be late for school.” Mrs. Holiday said, giving her daughter a quick kiss on the forehead. Barbie did as she was told, and grudgingly got ready and left for school.

“Look at that nerdy looking girl over there” Barbie snickered, pointing at skinny little girl with glasses and braces. Lily and Blanca laughed with her. They were her two slightly less pretty best friends. ”Look at that porky fat kid eating the doughnut.” Lily joined. Lily had red curly hair and was shorter, and a little plumper than Barbie. “Yeah, and look at his friend. Does he really think emo is in?” Blanca added, snootily. “The world sure is full of ugly people. Luckily we are not in that category. All those losers deserve to be made fun of. My theory is if you don’t take care of yourself you’re fair game. Those poor slobs, they don’t belong” Barbie finished. “Falling asleep in class already, Ms. Holiday. Not the best way to start off at a new school.” Said a loud booming voice out of nowhere. Barbie quickly snapped out of it. She had fallen asleep in class. “Look, she’s drooling” a pretty looking girl sitting to her right called out. Barbie’s face turned red out of embarrassment. “Let’s not let it happen again. We can’t have lazy people dragging us down, now can we?” The math teacher said. Barbie was in shock that a teacher, of all people, would speak that way to her. She sat in her seat quietly keeping to herself for the rest of the period. As she sat she looked at her classmates. They all had flawless skin, perfect hair, and not one of them was flabby or fat. The girls all had big boobs and small waists, and the guys were all muscular and trim. Even the teacher was attractive. Was this a school full of models, or what? When it was lunch time Barbie sat alone with her tray. She was deep in thought about how even the lunch lady was pretty, when someone tapped her on the shoulder. She turned to see that it was that girl who called her on her drool earlier in class. "You're in my spot" she said, crossing her arms over her rather large chest. "I didn't know our seats were assigned" Barbie replied sarcastically, not getting up. "Listen trailer trash, around here we do things a certain way. The ugly people go sit in the back next to the trash cans. They don't speak, unless spoken to. You don't belong." The girl icily retorted. She had steel blue eyes that were cold and hard, Wavy brown hair, and the body of a playboy bunny. "Barbie was taken aback by the girls comment. Everyone was looking at her now. They all looked so beautiful but so mean. Their eyes burned into her making her feel naked and insecure for the first time in her life. "Look she's gonna cry" a boy with black hair said, laughing. Barbie wouldn't give them that satisfaction, so before she burst into tears she split. How could they be so mean to her? Who were they to judge her? Never once did it cross her mind that she used to be exactly the same way.

The next couple of weeks were torture. No one was nice to her at school. The only time anyone even spoke to her was when they were making fun of her. Poor Barbie was all alone. Her mother had joined a women's bridge club and her father was always working. Barbie was completely isolated. For the first time in her perfect life, she was having it hard. As she walking down the street she took notice of her surroundings. Everyone was so beautiful here. Everyone was so perfect. She was lost in her own thought process so she didn't notice the garbage truck pull up next to her. She was so startled to see it that she tripped and fell. She landed in a pile of trash. "Move it lady. Can't you see that I'm trying to work?" Barbie looked up to see a hansom man mid thirties glowering over her. He had sandy blonde hair and muscular arms. He looked like he should be in the movies, not moving trash. Barbie quickly rose to her feet and picked the stray particles of trash off her dress. What is it with this town and everyone looking like super models? Were there no normal looking people here, or what? Barbie continued her walk and ended up at a small out door café. As she sat at her table she noticed a mother fussing with her daughter. The little girl was about six and kind of chunky. She could over hear the mother criticizing her child. "Amanda, you're so fat. You're never going to be beautiful if you keep eating cake. Look, you're getting a blemish. It's embarrassing to be seen out public with you." Barbie was shocked and the little girl looked as if she were about to cry. What is wrong with these people? Everyone was so concerned with how they looked. "Why hello there, I've never seen you here before" Barbie looked up from her late' to see the most strikingly hansom man standing over her. He had jet black hair and crystal blue eyes. He was tall and built with cute little dimples in his cheeks. She was so shocked that someone was being nice to her that she just starred at him with her mouth open. "You better close your mouth, or else the flies will get in" He said grinning. Barbie shut her mouth. "My name is Damon, and I couldn't help but notice that you were here all by yourself. May I join you?" he said reaching his hand out to her. She kissed his hand which made him laugh and her die of embarrassment. "I'm sorry, I have no idea why I just did that" Barbie sputtered; face growing redder by the minute. "It's cool. Surprisingly, this isn't the first time that's happened." He replied casually. "I'm Barbie. Please sit down." Barbie said finally smiling. "Pleased to meet you Barbie. But why is a gorgeous young woman like you doing all by herself?" he said as he took a seat next to her. "I don't seem to fit in, in this town. You're honestly the first and only person who has been nice to me." Barbie explained. "Well that's a shame. The people of this town don't know what they're missing. You're a doll." Damon said grinning. Barbie was so happy to finally have a friend. She was really staring to relax, when her cell phone rang. Barbie saw that it was her mother calling so she politely excused herself and answered her phone. "Barbie, get your fat ass home this instant. Your father and I need to have a serious talk with you." Her mom's voice nearly shrieked over the phone. Barbie was speechless. Why was her mother speaking to her that way? She quickly said goodbye to Damon and ran all the way home. Before she left however she exchanged phone numbers with the hansom stranger. What is she? Stupid? Of course she got his number.

When she arrived home she found her parents sitting on the couch. But to her shock, her parents looked completely different. Her mother went from plain to completely breathtaking. Her father did too. Her mother looked like a brunet version of Marylyn Monroe. Her father had re grown all his hair and looked dashing and debonair. “What happened to you two?” Barbie asked in shock. “That doesn’t matter. What matters is that you are too ugly for this family and we are sending you away” Mrs. Holiday said calmly while crossing and then uncrossing her now beautiful and shapely legs. “WHAT?!!” Barbie was dumbstruck. “Yes, your mother and I have decided that we can no longer tolerate someone with your unkempt appearance here in this household. What would the neighbors think? How would we explain you to our friends?” Mr. Holiday continued. “Mom, dad what’s wrong with you? I’m your daughter, how can you treat me this way? Where will I go?” Barbie cried nearly in tears. “You’re going to live with your Uncle Irving and Aunt Ida in Omaha. You’ll fit in better there on the farm, with the pigs. That way we won’t have to look at you. Pack your bags. Your plane leaves tomorrow morning.” Mrs. Holiday said. “Go to your room. We’re tired of looking at you. Your face disgusts us. Leave.” Mr. Holliday Bellowed. Barbie ran to her room with tears in her eyes. How could they treat her like this? Why were her parents being so mean? What on earth is going on? Barbie threw herself on her bed and cried for an hour. She finally fell asleep. She woke up at midnight to a strange sound coming from her parent’s room. When she peeked into their room she couldn’t believe what she saw. Her parents were glowing with what looked like some kind of smoke emitting from they’re mouths. Barbie screamed out of shock. She grabbed her phone and bolted out the door. She had nowhere to go and nowhere to turn. Just then she remembered her new friend. She quickly called him up. “Damon please I need your help” she hysterically screamed into the phone. “Barbie, what’s wrong? What’s going on?” Damon asked with concern. It occurred to her that she didn’t even know herself. “Can you pick me up please? I need you.” Barbie begged. “Sure, I’ll be right there” he replied. She gave him quick directions to her house and soon he pulled up in his 2009 jag. She didn’t really have time to awe over the car, so she jumped right in and they took off.

They stopped on top of a hill. “What’s wrong Barbie?” Damon asked with concern. “It’s terrible. My parents were so mean to me. Then, they were all glowing and crazy looking. It was so scary." Barbie said with a shiver. "Your parents, along with almost everyone in this town are losing their souls." Damon said calmly. "What are you talking about Damon?" Barbie questioned. "Your parents made a simple deal. Eternal life and beauty for their unholy souls." Damon answered. "What? How do you know all this?" Barbie asked, more than a little freaked. "I know all this because..." Damon paused for effect. "Because they made the deal with me." Damon finished, giving her a sinister grin. "Everyone who comes here ends up making the deal. Now all I need is you Barbie. What do you say? Do you want to be young and beautiful forever?" Damon asked reaching his hand toward her.

A year has passed in Lovely Lake and everyone is Beautiful. Barbie is back to being popular and everyone is happy. Of coarse she took the deal. She is blonde after all.

THE TALE OF THE DREAM WORLD REFUGEE

I've had the same dream since I was a little girl. I always wake up confused and disoriented because I am not where I fell asleep. One time I woke up in my neighbor's tree house. My dreams always seem so real, but this one in particular bothers me the most. It starts off that I'm in a strange land. I walk through an empty town, and there are signs everywhere with the same symbol printed on them. It looks somewhat like an eye within an eye. It's very creepy. As I walk through the town I actually feel the night air. It's damp and chilly outside and I go to a clock tower. The big hand points to twelve and the little one to three. I assume that it is three in the morning because it's dark out. Dugh! The clock bell clangs three times. On the third time I am surrounded by many people. They are all cloaked in midnight blue robes. Their faces are hidden with the hoods on their heads. They all reach out to me, trying to touch me. It's very scary. Then, a man from the crowd steps up in front. I only assume he's a man though, because he's so tall. I can't see his face but I think he's the one in charge. It's weird but I can almost feel his presence. It's very strong and it scares me. "We're waiting for you" he whispers. He I yell at my calico cat. She knocked over a vase. I always wake up at the same time. Yup, it's three fifteen in the freaking morning. I never get to finish the dream. I go and clean up the mess of glass and roses. It's Valentine's Day and I have no boyfriend to speak of. That's probably because I'm gay, but I don't have a girlfriend either. My ex and I broke up two weeks ago, so I bought the roses for myself. Happy Valentine's Day to me, whatever. I don't really care. I had been with her a year. She said she couldn't take my sleep habits. According to her I sleep walk and sleep talk almost every night. I think she just wanted to fuck the neighbor without a guilty conscience. I never woke up with her next to me, the whore. But sadly that's how all my relationships end. I guess I really do have a problem. I need to pick girls who are heavy sleepers and loyal. Yup, that's what I need to do alright. But seriously I have had this problem since, well as long as I can remember actually. I grew up in foster homes. My birth parents left me on the doorstep of a church, or so I'm told. I never made an effort to find my real parents because I figure if they didn't want me then, they sure as hell don't want me now.

Ugh, another boring day at work. I'm a telephone operator for the 'Voice Your Complains Department'. All day long I get to hear everyone's complaints. Does anyone care about mine? Nope. Scotty, the acne faced loser in the booth next to me comes over and snickers. "What's wrong? The lady on line two giving you trouble?" Oh my God he is so annoying. "No, I'm finished with her. Thanks for passing that bitch on to me by the way. Real lively, that one. I'm about to go on break." "You can't go on break yet. There's one more call for you. And you have to take it because they asked for you specifically." Scotty said as he transferred me the call and turned his flat ass to me and walked away. "Great" I mumble to myself. "Hello Complains Department. How may I help you?" I say in my fake telephone operator voice. "You don't belong here" the voice at the other end says. "Excuse me" I answer slightly taken aback. "Come home Rosalyn. We are waiting for you." And then there was silence. Whoa, I am speechless. That guy sounded like the guy from my dream. I take my headset off and find my way out of the building. Forget about taking a break. I need a day off. Seriously.

I'm waiting at the buss stop and notice a girl carrying a lot of bags. She manages for a while but then drops them all over the sidewalk. I feel sorry for her and offer my assistance. I take a moment to look at her and notice that she is very pretty. She has chin length black hair and bright blue eyes. "Thanks for helping me, my name is Jade." She says as she stands up and steady's herself. "Hi, no problem. My name is Ross." She starts to walk off and then stops and turns around. "This my sound a little forward, but can I buy you a drink?" she asks me with those big blue eyes. "I'm sorry but I gave up drinking" I say apologetically. "Oh, then here. Take this." She says handing me a pineapple. "What is this" I almost laugh. "It's a thank you present for helping me. I was at the Farmers Market and bought a bunch of fruit. I wanted to repay your kindness in some way." She says. I am honestly touched. "I don't drink, but I do eat. Can I buy you dinner sometime?" I don't know why my heart is beating so fast. I think I really like this girl. She pauses before she answers, then smiles coyly. "Sure I'm free tonight. Pick me up at eight." She gives me her address and we go our separate ways. Wow that was an interesting encounter.

Its seven fifty five and I'm at her place. She lives on the sixth floor of a high rise apartment complex. I don't know why, but I'm really nervous. I knock at her door and a large fat man answers. "Can I help you" He bellows. I'm kind of freaked out am about to leave when I get a tap on the shoulder. I turn around and see her standing there smiling. "You got the wrong place. Sorry, the doors aren't numbered." She says. I let out a sigh of relief. "Where do you want to go?" I ask. "I now this great little Italian restaurant just down the street. " she answers. As we walk to the restaurant we get to talking. I tell her my sad story. And she tells me about how she's half German half Japanese. I tell her about my dreams and she seemed to really understand. We get to the place and have a really great time. I've never opened up this much to someone I just met. There's just something about her. As I walk her home we make plans to go to the movies the next night. When I get to the door she stops. She looks at me and bluntly asks "Do you want to kiss me?" I am utterly shocked at her bluntness. She takes my silence as a yes and tilts her head up to my face. She gives me a soft, but loving kiss on the lips. "I thought so. Goodnight, see you tomorrow." She says as she walks into her apartment leaving me in the hallway, completely breathless.

I'm back at that empty town. The same symbol is everywhere. I get to the clock tower, but unlike before there is only one person there. He steps over to me. His presence is overwhelming. "When will you return Rosalyn? We're waiting for you." He reaches over and puts his hands on my face. I wake up with a start. It's three fifteen and my body is shaking. Why do I keep on having these dreams? What's wrong with me? How do these people know me? I go back to sleep, but sleep restlessly. The next few months seem to fly by. I'm still at that boring job. Scotty got promoted. Jade and I have been going steady and I am really happy. I'm thinking of asking her to marry me, but I haven't got up the courage yet. There's a knock at my door. I think it's Jade but it's not. It's actually two hooded figures that grab me and pull me inside. They pull out a syringe and stick it in my arm. They cover my mouth so I can't scream. As I drift off into the unconscious I hear them say "Now she's back where she belongs".

I'm in their world now. I'm not dreaming. I think I might be dead. I run through the deserted town yelling for help. I reach the clock tower and see the midnight blue robes. I try to run in the opposite direction but my body won't stop moving toward them. I see the leader. He beckons for me to come to him. "Your finally home" He says in his deep raspy voice. "What are you talking about? Who are you people?"I scream. "We are your family Rosalyn. Your one of us" The hooded figure replies. "No, it can't be. This can't be real." I'm in tears now. "We are real. Your parents sent you away when you were born. They were trying to give you a better life. They were punished accordingly." The man says. I look and see statues of a man and woman frozen in time. Their faces were contorted with pain and fear. I am really scared now. I need to wake up. Please let me wake up from this nightmare. "This is no nightmare Rosalyn. We are the dream weavers. We are where the nightmares come from." The man whispers sinisterly. I just want to wake up. "Where am I? What is this place?" I cry. "This is dream world. It's a parallel universe like the one you grew up in. You were never meant to leave." The man slowly removes his cloak. He has that symbol on his forehead. He touches my right arm and I feel a searing pain. I look to see that symbol branded on my skin. I am one of them. This is where I belong. I'm giving in but then hear a voice in the distance. "Ross, wake up. Please wake up." The voice in the distance says. Is that Jade? "Jade I'm here, help me please!" I cry. "You can never be rid of us, We will always be with you" The man yells. No, I have to wake up. I have to get back to Jade. I gather all my strength and scream at the top of my lungs. I open my arms and am in Jade's arms. "I thought I lost you" she cried with tears running down her face. "Where am I?" I ask out loud. "You're in your apartment. I came to see you and the door was open. You were on the floor. I thought you were dead." Jade replied hugging me to her. I feel better and I just lay there with her holding me. Then I notice something funny about her. She has a strange symbol on her chest. It's an eye within an eye. "Oh Shit" I say as I look up at her. "We are always with you" she says smiling. Then everything goes black.

THE FORGOTTEN VALENTINE

As life goes on and time drifts by forever seems like an eternity... Are you serious? This stuff is so lame. I hate English class. Boring. This day seems like an eternity. My name is Elizabeth Burrows. Liz for short. I'm seventeen and am a typical teenage girl. I have a long term boyfriend of four years named Thomas, badass friends, and a really cool hobby for acting. I'm thinking about being in a play. My best friend is Abby Benson. She's so cool. We've been friends since we were like two. She was the one who got me into acting. When we were younger we would put on plays together. My favorite was Romeo and Juliet. I drank caster oil in replace of poison and threw up all over the stage aka. The living room. It was awesome. Abby's memories are not as happy because she got some of my puke on her face. But she handled it like a real pro. She just started laughing then passed out. Too much caffeine I think, she's really fond of that Big Red. I prefer Dr.Pepper. Anyway, my drama teacher wrote a play called The Forgotten Valentine. She's going to begin casting it soon. I bet Abby and I can get the lead. We always do, we're the best in the class.

Casting session

Okay, the good news is Abby and I both got lead rolls. The weird news is we are playing star crossed lesbian lovers in a long distance committed long term relationship taking place in France and London. I play a French prostitute who is in love with her childhood sweetheart who has moved to England to become a nun. It's a weird story. I think my teacher was totally fucked up when she wrote it. She's so cool. She was nearly fired for allegedly smoking pot in the teachers lounge, but got off because she blew the vice principal for about an hour. That's the rumor anyway. "Well Abs, it looks like we're gonna have to kiss." I joke as I pretend to grab for her. "Please" she laughs "Do you really think you're the first girl I've kissed" "Wow, are you serious" I am completely confused, bothered and bewildered. I am also a bit hurt. Why wouldn't she tell me about her secret life of kissing women...and why didn't she want me to be her first kiss. Whoa, I can't believe I actually just thought that about my friend. I am totally losing it. I look over at her and can't help but grin. She's wearing her moms blue floppy beach hat and is dancing alone in the hallway to no music. She pauses to look at me and then shrugs her shoulders. "What, it's Tuesday" she says, and then keeps on dancing. Tuesday is dance day in case you're wondering. We've done it since we were like five. I join in, and after do*ing the robot, the funky chicken, the twist and the slide we finally stop. "Come on, we better get to class" I say. "See you at lunch" she replies as she gives me a quick hug and then runs off down the hallway. I stand there for a second watching her hop down the hall. She is literally hopping by the way. She does that sometimes. I smile, and for some reason find myself thinking about how good she smells. Weird.*

Lunch time at the Cafeteria

"Stop it Tommy, I'm trying to eat" I say as push my boyfriend off me. I normally don't mind it when he dry humps me and makes out with my ear in public, but for some reason I'm just not in the mood. "Get a room you two" Abby says as she rolls her eyes and plops herself down next to me. "Jealous baby, you know you can get some. All you have to do is ask" Tommy slurs. He's been binge drinking in the locker room again. "Yes Thomas, I am insanely jealous. I'm in love with you, you beast. You make me so hot, oh baby" Abby purrs crawling across the table. Her boobs are literally, like two inches from his face now. He's salivating and looks somewhat like a drunk cow. It looks like she is about to kiss him when she suddenly shoves his face into his macaroni. "Quit lusting after me, you sick pig. You're dating my best friend. Have more respect for her. Be a gentleman, God. You're pathetic." She then gets up, winks at me then leaves. I love it when she goes off like that. She did it just the other day to a homeless guy at the bus stop. "Gross, your pants are wet. Go change you perve." I say, giving him a flick on the ear. He is honestly too much sometimes. Sometimes I don't know why I'm even with him. Men. Jesus Christ.

Play Practice

“Sicily, I’m in love with you damn it. I have been ever since the day we met when you were selling flowers” Abby dramatically says to me while batting her long eyelashes. “Umm, correction if you please. It’s actually ‘the day you sold me your flower’ she’s a prostitute remember. Good job though Abby. Now grab her and kiss her.” Ms. Blake interrupts. I honestly think she gets off on this shit. I laugh nervously and look at my friend. She catches my eye then smiles. “Close your eyes. There’s no need to be nervous. It’s still me” she says stepping closer. I gulp. I don’t know why I’m so nervous. It’s just Abby. Yes, good old platonic best friend and nothing more Abby. Oh God, she smells so good. And then her lips hit me. It felt like time had literally stopped. It was just me and her. Her lips were on mine. Her soft, warm body pressed against me as her tongue tenitively slipped between my lips. I moan slightly and wrap my arms around her neck. “Fuck yeah bitches, do your thing. I’m getting a massive boner” some deush cat calls to us completely ruining the moment. “Fuck you, you gross perverted bastard. This is just acting” Abby lashes back, flipping off the guy in the front row. Of coarse it’s just acting. I was crazy to think it was anything more. Damn it to hell, I feel like such a fool. Ahhhh!!! I want to die.

It’s been a little over a week since ‘the kiss’. Business has continued on as usual. Abby’s acting like it never happened, so why should I be making a big deal of it. It was nothing, just a meaningless stage kiss for the sake of theater. It doesn’t matter that her lips are soft and luscious, or that they taste like cherries. She’s a girl, my very best friend for that matter and I am totally and completely strait. Were her boobs always that perky or is it the blouse? Ahhh!! Mind out of the gutter Lizzie, think of your boyfriend. Think of Tommy. I turn to look at my hansom prince. He’s eating a chili dog, and has cheese on his shirt. How…ummm…very…sexy. “Let’s have sex” I say as I look at him in the eye. “What, now? Hell yeah baby, meet me in the janitors closet” He nearly squeals, already beginning to disrobe. “Not now. And are you fucking serious, the janitor’s closet, for real. I want our first time to be special. And it smells like throw up in there.” I say, beginning to feel like I had just made a huge mistake. “Fine, whatever, meet me at my house after school. I promise you a deflowering you will never forget." He says as he kisses me on my forehead and then walks off. I hope I know what I'm doing. I really hope I don't regret this.

Deflowering session Tommy's room

Okay, this is definitely not what I had in mind. I'm lying on Tommy's bed with nothing but a tee-shirt on. One of his I might add. It kind of smells. His room is actually the down stairs basement. It's creepy and cold down here, and I swear I just heard a rat squeak. I'm just about to get up and run when the love of my life walks in, in nothing but a pair of old boxers. "Are you ready to become a woman baby girl" he drawls, coming over to the bed. "Yes" I manage to squeak. I am so nervous I feel like I'm about to puke. He climbs on top of me and begins to kiss me. His kisses are rough and his lips are dry. His face is prickly because he hasn't shaved in a couple of days. I feel something hard poking into me. Dear Lord, I hope that's his finger. But unfortunately it wasn't his finger, nor was it his knee. He pulled out his thing and I no longer have much of an appetite for corn dogs. "Don't worry baby, the first time always hurts but I promise it gets better." He purrs while kissing my ear. "How very reassuring. Look, it's getting late and I have a ton of homework to do. So, why don't we continue this on another day." I say as I quickly roll off the bed and stand up. "Are you serious. I've waited around for you for four fucking years without so much as a blow job, and you pull this shit with me. I have blue balls damn it. Give me some or it's over" he angrily shouts. "Is that all our relationship is to you. Just trying to get laid. Is that all that I am to you Tommy. Just a good fuck" I'm pissed now. "I wouldn't know now would I. I never have actually fucked you now have I? You keep your legs closed do damn tight, I wonder if you even have a pussy" I slap him at that point, really hard. He steps back a bit then smirks. He's about to make another smart ass remark when I flick him off and walk out. How dare he act that way with me. I can't believe I wasted so much of my time on him. He's such a jerk. I'm glad it's over. Now I know. It's better this way. I need ice cream.

I am so depressed. I run all the way to Abby's house. Her mom lets me in and I go up to her room. I hear some strange noises coming from behind the door but think nothing of it. I walk right in like I always have and come to a shocking discovery. Abby is lying half naked on her bed with some girl I have never seen before just coming up from what I assume was giving her head. I feel like a million knives are hitting my heart as a ton of bricks hit my face. Abby see's me and sit's up real quick, covering herself with a blanket. "What the fuck Liz. What are you doing here" she gasps. "Leaving" I say as I run out the door and nearly trip down the stairs on my way out. I don't know why I'm so hurt. It's not like I'm in love with her or anything. Please, that would be crazy. Me, in love with Abby; that's absurd. I go strait to my room when I get home. I cry for a little over an hour, but I don't really know why. I just need to get some sleep. Tomorrow will be better, I hope.

The next day I avoid Tommy and Abby. I eat alone outside. I still don't know why I'm being so anti social. As I go to my locker I notice that what looks like a piece of paper is shoved into it. I pick it up and see that it's a note in the shape of a heart. It simply says 'I love you. I'm sorry' printed on it in big bold letters. Tommy must have sent it. Poor bastard still thinks he has a chance. I go look for him to set him strait, and find him in the gym. "Nice try with the note. But too little too late. We're through." I call out as I walk up to him. "What the hell are you talking about, you crazy woman" he asks seeming genuinely confused. Wait a minute. If he didn't write the note, then who did? I have no time for this, so I walk out without even answering him. I am so confused, but have no time to worry about it. The play is tonight so I have to practice.

The opening act

I am so nervous. Not really about the actual play but more about what goes on in it. The kiss is very nerve wrecking. I begin to calm down and get into the play until the scene that I've been dreading comes up. "Sicily, I'm in love with you" Abby says coming up to me. I am about to answer when she suddenly interrupts. "Did you get my note" she asks eyes wide and hopeful. "Wait, that was you" I am now totally and officially confused. "Of coarse it was me. Who else would it be" She comes closer. "Lizzi, I'm sorry you had to see me like that. I honestly wished that it had been you on me and not her" My mouth is open and I am still in shock. Did I just hear what I thought I just heard? Abby wastes no time and quickly grabs me by the waist and gives me the longest, hottest, most passionate kiss I have ever had. My knees go week and I nearly fall but she catches me. "I love you Lizzi. I have since we were like twelve. You're my girl. You're the one that I want. I always have and always will. I want you." Abby is looking at me in a way that makes me feel naked and safe at the same time. "I love you too" I breathe, and we kiss again. We would have totally had sex in the middle of the stage if some retard didn't' throw popcorn at us. We didn't care though. We blew that popsicle stand real quick, not even bothering to finish up the play. That was the best night of my life. That was the night I fell in love. That was the night I first made love. That was the night I got my first girlfriend. I finally found love. I'm glad it was her. We still dance on Tuesdays. Although now there's more than just us dancing. We have an eight year old daughter named Mickey Jane, a two year old son named Robert and twins on the way. Who says lesbians can't have families. I love my wife and she loves me. We're a happy family. We'll be together till the end of time. Because there will never be again a forgotten valentine.

Authors note

I wish my life was like my stories. I have yet to find my true love. I'm twenty one years old so I guess there's still time. I find myself a little bit alike to both Abby and Lizzie. I'm comfortable with my sexuality like Abby. I'm GAP (Gay And Proud). I am also insecure like Lizzie, because I too am in love with my best friend. Love is hard especially when you're young. Actually, love is hard period. What makes love work is a lot of communication. You need to be honest with your partner. But, more importantly be honest with yourself. Love is beautiful. But, love is also scary, confusing, and hurtful. Love can make you or break you. It's very powerful. To love you do not have to conform. Gay love is Just as beautiful as strait love. I don't care what people say. There is, was, and never will be anything wrong with being gay. Be yourself and love whoever you want to love. Then maybe some day life will be like my stories. Maybe some day everyone will find true love, and everyone will have a happy ending.

www.ingramcontent.com/pod-product-compliance
Ingram Content Group UK Ltd.
Pitfield, Milton Keynes, MK11 3LW, UK
UKHW051133260726
13967UKWH00010B/3017